Borne

Asta Horne

Copyright

Dedication

This book is dedicated to every person who felt like a stranger in their own skin.

Based on True Events

Many of the situations you will read about in the Shadow Borne series are based on true events from the author's life. Growing up with paranormal 'gifts' wasn't always easy, but it was never boring either.

More by Asta Horne

1. https://www.amazon.com/Awaken-Shadow-Borne-Book-1-ebook/dp/B0C1L21J8S

COMING SOON

TO KEEP UP WITH SHADOW Borne and upcoming series, please follow Asta on:

<u>Instagram</u>[2]
<u>TikTok</u>[3]
<u>Facebook</u>[4]

---

2.   https://www.instagram.com/practicallypsychic/

3.   https://www.tiktok.com/@astahorne

4.   https://www.facebook.com/profile.php?id=100087678257774

Prologue

White light crashes overhead as Ellice Craig ducks behind the nearest car. The world dulls in its wake. Sound and sensation both fray, leaving her exposed.

No no no no no.

High Priestess Aldora's voice booms from everywhere at once. "The Goddess has spoken. Return what is ours and you shall live."

Another bright light explodes, nearer this time. Ellice uses the chance to search for cover up ahead. Overturned cars burn around her. Everything is closing in.

In the distance, there's a small building like an electrical shed. It's probably the worst place to hide, aside from this flimsy Prius that could fly away at any moment.

"Come out before this entire city burns!" This time it's High Priest Draigh's deafening howl that cuts through the night.

The whole world will burn before I let you win.

Ellice looks at her bandaged hands, willing them to work one last time. She stretches her aching fingers but nothing happens.

Absently, Ellie feels for the bundle she'd had strapped to her chest. But it's gone. She *knew* it would be, but still she couldn't stop herself from checking. Always checking in hopes that she was wrong.

No, the bundle is gone now, along with everything else she once held dear.

The next flash of light is tinged with red as it nearly finds its mark. Ellie knows she must run for the building now. But she's frozen.

Where is he?

All she sees is smoke and fire, but he has to be out there. Somewhere. *Please...*

Ellice doesn't know if she's begging him, or the Goddess, or her damn hands. But these damn hands are the only thing she currently has some control over.

ELLICE PUSHES BACK against the car, desperately molding her body to its form.

Blood thrums in her head as she forces a calming breath, then another. On the third, she unwraps the scrap of his bloody t-shirt from her hands. The pain explodes as burnt flesh tears away with it.

Biting her lip to keep from screaming, she kisses the shirt before letting it drop to the road. It may be the last thing of his she'll ever touch.

Aldora's voice reverberates in Ellice's chest. "I shall not ask again!" She's getting closer. Another blinding flash of white illuminates the sky.

Ellice takes the opportunity to search for him, but to no avail.

I've lost everything. But they won't take me alive.

She returns to her breathing, starting over with one, two, three. She must make it to five. On the fourth, the familiar warm blue glow begins to creep down her forearm.

As smoke fills her lungs on the fifth breath, Ellice rises to her feet and calls out to the darkness. "Your reign is over! There is nothing left for any of us. I'll see you in Hell!"

Ellice's palms burn as lightning crackles within them.

I'm sorry I failed you.

Ellice clasps both hands over her heart.

And as the pulse of electricity begins to charge, a large hand clamps down on her shoulder.

Chapter One

Ellice Craig was never a good girl, per se. Growing up in a strict Scottish Catholic household, how could one live up to the standards of the Lord Almighty?

By twelve she knew it was all horse shit.

By fifteen, she'd built up the courage to tell her mother so.

And by fifteen plus one day, she was homeless.

But that suited Ellice just fine. She had Cora now.

Coraline Montrose was heir to a tobacco fortune, or so she told anyone who was fool enough to listen. But Ellice knew from her first night on Skid Row—a dangerous place she'd heard of but thought only a cautionary tale for wayward children—she knew the truth in Cora's heart. The barely thirteen year old girl was more lonely than Ellice had ever been.

Cora was also the only thing keeping Ellice alive those first two years.

You see, Ellice had a gift. Several, in fact, as she would later learn. But for now, Ellice had *a* gift. The Sight, as her also excommunicated Granda Marian had put it.

With this Sight, Ellice knew at once what was horse shit and when someone was lying. Oftentimes, as with her parents, Ellice also knew when a person was lying to themselves. She never faulted them for their beliefs. On the contrary, she often wished her life could be so simple. They'd only just come over from Scotland before falling pregnant with Ellice, their supposed miracle child who finally showed up just as they'd resigned themselves to being childless. A fat load of good that did her fifteen years later!

No, Ellice never faulted, but never forgave either. Not only for being cast out on the street, but for every horrid thing she'd had to endure under their god's eye. Spare the rod and all.

Now, at the ripe old age of eighteen, after saving every penny from her three years working under the table at the video store, she was able to rent a closet-sized apartment for herself and her 'little sister' Coraline Montrose. The regal name, which she'd used for both of them on the lease, had aided the landlord in overlooking the fact that the 'sisters' looked nothing alike.

Where Cora was tall and thin with the golden hair of a fairy princess, Ellice was more short and less thin with the fiery hair of a leprechaun. And the accent to boot.

So, it was in that tiny apartment the two young women thrived. Cora somehow stayed rail thin whereas Ellice's curves began to take shape into something her parents would have hated.

Would serve them right to see me now.

But she had no intention of that ever happening.

It was also in that tiny apartment where Cora urged Ellice to use her Gifts. Sometimes for good and sometimes for... less good. Although, the worst thing Ellice could bring herself to do was read the thoughts of a certain young man she noticed on the subway one morning.

He was the only other person she'd ever seen with hair as red as hers. She'd always thought she would hate seeing it on a man, but she found she did not. In fact, she often found herself wondering if he would have the same thick Scottish accent she'd inherited from her parents, despite the fact of never once setting foot on its green soil.

So, upon reading the handsome young man's thoughts and finding that he considered her the most beautiful woman *he'd* ever seen, of course she started choosing seats closer and closer to his.

Until one day, she was left with no other recourse than to put out her hand and ask, "Is this seat taken?" She swallowed the last word, sure her accent would scare him off.

The man, clearly in shock, only shook his head as his cheeks flushed the same color as their hair. Ellice found it endearing, and sexy, though it masked the two freckles she'd admired from afar for all these few weeks.

Still, something nagged at the back of her mind as they chatted.

"I-I'm Jonah. Croft. Jonah Croft!" he finally said after the train had resumed moving.

"Ellice," she said, offering her hand again. "Sounds like Alice... if yer wonderin'." Which he was.

This time he took it, and literal sparks flew.

They both jumped, but neither released the other's hand.

Damn Cora making me practice so much.

"Ellie, such a pretty name. Irish?"

She did not correct him, other than to whisper, "Scottish" with that damned thick lilt. One can't say any word related to her distant homeland without fully leaning into it.

Ellie...

She let the name roll off the tongue of her mind and found she quite liked it.

Nobody called her Ellie in her life. Her parents 'named her Ellice for a reason' and Cora found 'Ellice' to be way too intriguing of a name to not use it. Besides, in her mind's eye, she envisioned him calling her that for the rest of his life, and she loved it. For him alone, she would be Ellie.

And yet.

Shaking the thought away, Ellie began grilling her companion. She knew she only had four more stops to make him hers.

"Where do you work?" She already knew the answer, of course. She didn't *spy* on him as one might call it. It wasn't her fault that she could just *see* things. And one of the things she'd seen was the glow about him every morning as he'd ascend the subway stairs and rush to the tall glass-faced building. Yes, she knew he loved his job and wanted to see him light up as he told her about it.

Which he did. "Emerson and Fielding. Sounds like a law office, I know. But it's actually a tech firm. We make computer mainframes." He stopped and bit his lip. "They're large boxes that house... well, computers. Only a few places use them now—a few Top Secret," he added with a wink, then another blush. "But Mr. Harrison, my boss says that pretty soon there will be one in every house if he has anything to say about it. I don't know if I believe him. They're so huge. I don't know where I'd put one in my little apartment." He cut off abruptly.

Ellie could tell he was embarrassed for rattling on like that, but she loved every second.

She could also tell, with a flash of her Sight, that indeed every household will have one... more than one. Even carry them around in their pockets and purses.

"Maybe they'll be smaller by then."

Jonah scrunched his cute little nose for a moment, then his eyes went wide. "Yes! That's brilliant! Can I steal that?"

"Sure." Ellie shrugged and glanced out the window. One more stop.

There was a brief awkward silence where all of a sudden Ellie didn't want to look away from the subway window. Didn't want to see the excitement and worry on Jonah's face as he worked up the courage to ask her out.

She knew it would cause so much pain to so many.

And she knew she'd say yes anyway.

Chapter Two

"Tell me everything!" Cora sat on the edge of the ratty old couch with her legs crossed under her. "I can't believe you finally did it!"

Now seventeen, Cora *could* go get a job of her own to help with the bills, but 'for now' Cora had declared her job to be training Ellice to harness her immense powers.

The girl had too much time on her hands to read every old comic book she could find.

"Not much to tell." Ellice stalled.

The last thing she needed was to worry Cora with her visions. Something about them troubled her deeply. For reasons she didn't yet understand, this future was hazy, unrefined. Her subconscious didn't want her to know what was coming and she didn't like it.

But most of all, not seeing Cora or feeling her presence in these flashes was terrifying.

What's coming?

"Don't you dare!" Cora squealed. "I've been waiting weeks for this moment. Let me live vicariously."

Well, if she won't go back to school at least she's reading those vocabulary books.

"Alright," Ellice said as she plopped onto the couch beside her little sister, for that's what they were now. And she let herself be carried away by the memory. "He was so adorable telling me all about his computer job. They're gonna be everywhere, you know? Everybody will have one in their pocket!"

Except for you.

Ellice slammed the metal doors in her mind shut to lock the thought out. Another trick Cora had read about in a psychic magazine that worked wonders, most of the time.

Cora's face was scrunched up and Ellice could see her mentally working out how to squish a giant black mainframe with blinking lights and hundreds of wires down to pocket-size.

Normally, Ellice wouldn't violate Cora's trust by peeking. She'd made a solemn vow. But this was fine. Cora was basically broadcasting her thoughts to the world. They'd both been working on their Mind Shields—Cora demanded that all things psychic be revered and warranted such capitalization—but in the privacy of their home, neither much bothered.

They had no secrets.

But one.

Ellice had known for a while now that Cora's life would be a short bright flash. And in the moments when those thoughts crept in, she was glad Cora couldn't read minds also.

"... what I'd do with one if I had it. I'm not a businessman." Cora had been speaking the whole time Ellice was lost in thought and she tried to catch up.

She closed her eyes and returned back to the memory. Funny calling the future a memory but that's what it felt like every time. "Games," she said after a moment. "Games and... talking to people."

Spying on people was the true eerie feeling she got, but no sense saying that either. It wouldn't matter to Cora, anyway.

Cora gasped and punched Ellice lightly on the arm. "Nice try. Don't change the subject. I want the juicy stuff?"

"Nothing juicy." She tried to sound appalled but Ellice couldn't hide the dreaminess in her voice. "We didn't get to talk long."

"Five stops."

Ellice nodded. "And he took one whole stop to finally speak! But..." She paused for dramatic effect. "He asked me out."

Cora squealed again but caught herself halfway and the rest was muffled by her clamped lips. "The Depot?"

"No, actually," she said slowly. "McAllister's."

"What do you think that means? Did you see it wrong? You've never been wrong before." Cora's brow furrowed as she chewed on the tip of her long hair.

Ellice's mind raced. The vision didn't *feel* wrong. So what changed?

That was it!

Her Sight only gave her *possible* futures. Things could change.

She could *make* them change!

She could save Cora!

Chapter Three

For the next six months, Ellice did nothing besides eat, sleep, and train.

And fall madly in love with Jonah.

Cora didn't ask why the sudden change in work ethic and Ellice left it that way.

Every night, after work—and lunch with Jonah and sometimes dinner—Ellice returned home to develop her skills. Cora also helped her unlock new ones.

So far she'd discovered that she had a modicum of control over nature. She used this power for good only, bringing sunshine and flowers to their doorstep every morning. No matter the weather in the rest of the city... or the fact that they lived on the third floor.

Ellice also found that she somehow knew impossible herb mixtures that would cure anything that ailed them. Including one time, an obviously broken toe from falling *up* the subway steps.

But most fun and frightening of all. Ellice found her Light.

One night after a long training session of trying to combine her other two Gifts by mending a forgotten bouquet of roses Cora found in the trash outside their building, Ellice's hands began to crackle.

As Cora's eyes went wide as saucers, Ellice's closed.

She remembered that morning on the subway with Jonah. The moment their hands touched, there had been a spark. One that felt oddly similar to this blue light in her palm now. She knew it was blue even through closed eyes. It *felt* blue.

"What the-" Cora whispered. (Ellice did not allow her to swear in the house, although she was fully an adult now, and often slipped up.)

Ellice opened her eyes. The blue crackle was now a blue orb, vibrating with such energy Ellice could contain it no longer. It shot forth, finding the nearest target—the poor bouquet she'd just succeeded in reviving.

Both women gasped and Ellice felt the life force of the roses shrivel. She knew there was no saving them now.

"I'm sorry."

"Are you kidding? That was *amazing*!"

It didn't feel amazing. She had vowed long ago to never use her power to destroy.

Ellice looked at her palms. The blue lightning had dissipated but still remained, somewhere deep within her. She didn't dare call it back.

"I know what you are..." Cora was still whispering, as if fully speaking would break the spell.

Spell?

Why did that word come to mind? Of all things?

"You're a witch!"

Yes!

"Nonsense!"

Cora ran to her room and returned a few seconds later with an old book. It was bound in something akin to leather, but had the aura of... something Ellice knew her mind couldn't handle at this moment. Being in the same room with it was hard enough. The thing felt like it wanted to suck out her soul.

How is Cora holding it so calmly?

"Here!" Cora said, ignoring everything and flipping to a page highly stuffed with sticky notes and marked with several different colors of ink.

The book didn't like it one bit and Ellice was nudged by something strong inside her to tell Cora so.

"Look!" Cora tapped her finger on a section of the creepy—*sorry*. The book didn't like that either. On the *antique* book. She read a quote out loud, though Ellice already knew what it would say. "She who holds the power of the elements at her fingertips and calls forth The Goddess within them shall be hereby deemed... a Witch."

The thing inside Ellice snapped into place. "I didn't call anything forth," she argued weakly.

"I knew it!" Cora ignored her pleas, for that's what they were. A plea to the universe or whatever intelligence there was above for this not to be happening to her. Not now. Not when she finally found happiness.

Cora paced the room, reading silently and muttering to herself. "I knew it. I didn't want to say anything until I was sure... with your past and all. But there's no denying it."

Ellice shook her head.

Please don't say it.

"Ellice Craig, ye be a Witch!" Cora giggled, but only for the length of one breath.

For that was how long it took the *ancient* book in her hand to slap itself shut and the room to go dark.

Cora and Ellice lunged for each other and huddled together, trembling in fear.

Cora wept in Ellice's arms. "I'm sorry. I'm so sorry. I-I don't know what I did."

"Nothing. You did nothing," Ellice lied.

She did the one thing that Ellice knew would doom them all.

Chapter Four

Two days their apartment had been plunged into darkness. The landlord and six different repair men had tried and failed to restore power to the unnaturally black and cold rooms.

Nothing else had happened after the book slammed itself shut and fell to the floor.

Nothing besides the light within the book—a light Ellie would later confirm that only she had seen—had fizzled out.

Oh, and the lightning that seemed to follow Ellie everywhere.

On the third day, Ellie worked up the courage to ask for help.

Cora, too, had decided to do something about their situation. Ellie could See that it was bad, but didn't violate Cora's trust by truly Seeing. She only waited for the fallout and hoped she'd know how to fix things by then.

How she would figure that out, she hadn't figured out. One thing was certain, though. Their apartment would never regain its light as long as she—or the book—remained there.

"I... uh... need a favor," she said to Jonah as they walked to McAllisters, *their spot.*

"Sure," Jonah answered brightly and squeezed her hand.

Ellie was nervous. For the first time in a while, she couldn't see the outcome of this conversation. She didn't *know* what would happen next, and it terrified her.

She could still See, of course, but not where Jonah was concerned. Whatever had happened to her that night had snatched away her ability to sense her own future. It was disorienting. Under normal circumstances, this would be exciting. A life of surprises. A *normal* life.

But given the way this change came about, *terrifying* was all Ellie could call it.

"Sure," Jonah said again with a more concerned tone of voice. He stopped walking and let go of her hand. Placing his palms on her cheeks, he kissed her gently on the forehead. "Anything for you, Ellie Bellie."

She should have hated that nickname but it always filled her chest with a warmth she knew home should have felt like.

"Our building's power went out the other day and they haven't gotten it back on. I... well, Cora and I... were wondering if..." She faltered.

Even without Gifts, Jonah knew what she was getting at.

And they both *knew* what it could mean for their relationship.

Until now, they'd kept things somewhat casual, yet not without that burning need that grows between a man and a woman who are destined for each other. Still, they'd yet to act upon it. Once that line was crossed, there was no turning back. And here she was asking for just that thing.

Jonah swallowed hard and his freckles disappeared. "S-Sure," he said again with less conviction. "You can—you *both* can come stay with me until it's figured out."

"Thank you," Ellie said as Jonah turned back to the sidewalk but didn't resume walking.

"It's only," he said sheepishly. "It's only one room. I don't even know if the couch folds out. But... but of course I'll sleep on it regardless. You can have the bedr—room."

Ellie floated through the afternoon unable to think about anything other than tonight.

Her world may be coming to an end, and she'd do everything in her power to stop that from happening.

Tomorrow.

"We don't have a choice," Cora said for the third time... at least the third that Ellice heard. The tone of her voice insinuated many more attempts to talk sense into her sister.

Ellice paced the small apartment with their last emergency candle, gathering the essentials. Her mind raced about everything, yet focused on none. Her budding powers. The damn book. Moving Cora out of her own room. Keeping her Gifts from Jonah. Her inability to See how revealing her power would affect their relationship. Tonight. Every night after.

Tonight.

Ellice and Cora had spent many years on Skid Row; a ruthless place, for sure. All those destitute people in one place, you're bound to have some crime. Some terrible acts of human depravity. But it had not been as dangerous for them as it could have been. Ellice had learned early on how to produce a bubble of protection around herself and her sister. And when they couldn't be physically together, Ellice had poured that white light into a cheap metal ring from one of those candy machines outside the local grocery store.

Yes, they'd lived a hard life in many respects, but still sheltered in one that mattered most to Ellice. If tonight became *the* night, as it most assuredly seemed to be heading, it would be her first. She smiled at the warm glow of anticipation—quickly followed by dread—building in her gut.

Cora snapped her fingers in Ellice's face. "How are you *smiling* right now... ohhhh." One side of her mouth quirked up in a grin. "But of course." She drew out the words like a cat purring.

"Stop it!"

"I'm happy to give you any pointers if you-"

"No!"

Cora hadn't been so chaste in their time on the streets. And especially since moving into the apartment. When your neighbors were two hot college guys, one could hardly blame her.

"Fine." Cora raised her hands and dropped them in exasperation. "And I'm all for you finally popping your cherry-"

"Ew."

"But right now we have to do something about that book." Cora pushed past Ellice.

"No!" Ellice yelled again, but for a much different reason.

After the first few hours had passed with no further harbingers of the apocalypse, they had picked the book up with salad tongs and placed it in a shoe box. Then wrapped the shoebox in a whole roll of masking tape and hid it in the back closet. Ellice didn't even know they had salad tongs but she was sure grateful they did.

But now, with her wits about her, she can't believe she put her sister in so much danger.

Cora stopped but only long enough for her to catch up. When she began to march toward the closet, Ellice grabbed her arm.

"I know we need to—I need to do this. But you aren't going anywhere near it. I'll do it." Ellice gave Cora her best 'big sister' look.

"That's so dumb. If something happens, we should both be there to absorb...whatever." Cora shrugged. "Four hands are better than two."

"And that's exactly why you can't touch it. I shouldn't have let you help the first time. If something happens, I should be the only one it happens to."

She wanted to add, 'because I can take it,' but they'd both know it was a lie.

Cora, not usually one for backing down, glared at Ellice before responding, "Do you really want to die a virgin?"

Ellice couldn't help but laugh. "Maybe."

"I promise you...you don't." Her glare turned to something playful. Then, after a moment, she huffed a sigh. "Fine, I won't touch it, but I'm not leaving."

Ellice counted that as a win and stepped past Cora.

When she opened the closet, the shoebox glowed like a beacon. She turned back to Cora who didn't seem to notice anything. Glowing or not, Ellice knew she'd never lose track of the ancient book. They were inextricably linked now. Forever.

Ellice bent over the shoe box and said a small prayer under her breath, not to any god, but to the Universe itself. "Please don't leave Cora an orphan."

The yellow glow emanating from the shoe box flickered, then expanded, turning white then blue.

She *knew* she could now hold the book itself, without the protection of the box or any other barrier. But she did not.

Ellice took the box under her arm, feeling her energy meld with that of the book inside, becoming One with the power that had formed her.

Seeing this, Cora clapped her hands. "Great! Now let's get you laid."

Chapter Five

The whole way to Jonah's apartment, Cora briefed Ellice on what might (or definitely would) go down that night.

What she should wear. How far up she should shave. What she could say. And much to Ellice's chagrin... What would go where.

Ellice knew all of this of course. One doesn't have the Gift of Sight without taking a peek at certain things. Out of scientific curiosity only, she told herself.

But she was happy to let Cora chatter on. She couldn't remember the last time her sister had been out of their apartment, even in its new state of being a black hole devoid of all things good.

That damned book.

By the time they got to Jonah's apartment and Ellice had knocked—with the help of Cora's hand holding her arm and making her—Cora was positively vibrating with the excitement they both felt.

Ellice's was more of a gnawing need to puke.. but also from excitement.

The door swung open as if Jonah had been staring out the peephole for the last five minutes.

Which Ellie *knew* he had.

"Come in," he said too loudly, then cleared his throat and tried again. "Come in. The...uh... room is over there." He pointed to an average looking door that led to the now scariest place Ellie could imagine. "And the bathroom's over there."

Cora ran to the easy chair in the living room and settled in. "Oh I've missed you," she cooed to the television.

Ellie knew Cora hated 'Gilligan's Island' but the girl didn't seem to care.

"Can I offer you a drink? Water! O-Or soda?" Jonah was sweating and his freckles had once again disappeared.

Over the television Cora gave Ellie a sly look which Ellie pretended not to see.

Could he be as nervous as I am? Sure he's...

Ellie decided she'd rather not know if he'd... and let him pour her a glass of water.

The three of them sat in near silence for two more Gilligans and a 'Murder She Wrote.' But when 'Bewitched' came on, Cora quickly changed the channel and Ellie jumped up.

She excused herself to the bathroom to hide her pounding heart.

When she returned, Cora and Jonah were arguing under their breath about something. Before Ellie could reach them, Cora plopped herself on the couch, grabbed the blanket Jonah had set out for himself, and refused to budge.

Jonah looked to Ellie with a combination of fear and... yes, hope.

Without a word, Ellie turned and walked to the bedroom.

When she dared to look back, Jonah was following close behind. The look in his eyes filled her with a very new kind of warmth.

JONAH KISSED ELLIE gently on her cheek, then her lips, her neck, and back to her lips.

They had been standing beside the bed for at least ten minutes, neither bold enough to initiate the move.

Ellie took a deep breath while Jonah returned to her neck and lowered herself onto the mattress. It was much softer than she'd imagined and she sank into it as Jonah's lips followed her down.

He pushed himself up onto his elbows and stared down at her. "I love you," he whispered.

"I love you, too." Tears burned the corners of Ellie's eyes.

They'd never said it before, though both of them had known for a while.

And now, with it out in the open, a calm settled over the room. They were in love and this was not a sin.

Ellie hated that the cloud of her childhood still hung over her sometimes, especially at this very inopportune time.

"Hey." Jonah tucked a finger under her chin and lifted her up to meet his gaze. "I love you," he said again.

This time, even without his own Sight, he knew what she was thinking and those three words were a promise that she would never know that sort of pain again.

"I love you more." Ellie pulled him down so her lips could graze his ear. "Until the world ends."

She didn't know why she had to put it that way, but soon it didn't matter.

Jonah's skin prickled under her fingertips and she felt a shiver run through his body.

"Are you sure?"

"Of course I'm sure," Ellie answered, almost indignant. Did he not believe her?

"No," Jonah said meekly, gesturing with his eyes to their impossibly close but not close enough bodies. Then more slowly, "Are you sure?"

With a wry grin Ellie pulled him down again and matching the deep need in Jonah's tone, she whispered, "Of course I'm sure."

They fumbled a bit at first, neither knowing quite where things went—despite Cora's best efforts to school her on the subject. Ellie knew then that no, surely he hadn't before.

Soon they settled into a slow, gentle rhythm. Kissing and caressing every part of each other. They found that if they shut their minds out of the process, their bodies *knew* what should come next.

Still, when she felt Jonah's hand slip between them and then under her panties, she couldn't help but gasp.

He pulled his hand out, but she grabbed his arm and guided him back down, rising to meet him in the process.

He was still shaking and began to tremble more when her own hand found his belt, then his zipper.

She became desperate then, yanking at the fabric, trying to get it off off... *off.*

Jonah tore himself away from her and stood at the foot of the bed, tearing at his clothes.

Ellie quickly slid hers off as well and scooted to the edge.

She wanted to see him. All of him.

He was more muscular than she'd imagined. He'd always seemed so trim in his suit and jacket. Earlier that evening, sitting so close on the couch in less formal attire, she'd tried and failed to feel what might be waiting for her. But now, beneath those layers she wished would never obscure him from her again, he was lithe and sensuous.

And, as her eyes trailed downward, captivating.

Though Ellie had never seen one, she didn't need to know what others looked like to know this was more than average. There was a moment of trepidation before the thought of them joining took over her senses. Her mind tried to prepare her, but she pushed all thought aside.

She wasn't sure how her body would accept such a thing, but she would damn sure try!

Jonah rushed to her with a fierce kiss and lifted her up into his arms. In one swift motion, he crawled to the head of the bed, carrying her easily with him.

"Stop me if anything... if you don't..." He was breathing heavily and Ellie wondered if he could stop now, if she wanted him to.

But she didn't.

"Shh," she whispered and inched herself forward.

Jonah closed the rest of the distance between them. Until there was none.

There was a tiny flash of pain that made her flinch, but it was soon replaced with the most intense fullness. And pleasure.

Oh yes, pleasure.

Every inch of her body buzzed with it.

They moved slowly at first, then as their need for each other rose to such great heights, the urgency took over. She moved in ways she never thought possible, writhing beneath him and pushing when he came to her.

It was like nothing she ever imagined. Being a virgin didn't mean she was a saint, and she'd thought of this moment since before she knew Jonah's name. But she'd never done him justice. This was more than she could bear and she wanted more.

When they could wait no longer, it exploded inside her like a volcano.

He fell onto her with his release and held her tight.

They both lay quiet, him still on top of her, neither wanting to be the one to end this.

When he finally rolled off her, Ellie was so spent she couldn't open her eyes.

She hadn't Seen anything like that!

Chapter Six

Ellice and Cora never returned home to their apartment, which, by the way, never regained power. Whatever had happened between her and the book had been permanent.

They did, once, go back for a brief afternoon to retrieve a few essentials. Nothing more than clothes and a few sentimental items they'd collected over the years. While there, Ellice risked peeking into Cora's mind to make sure there were no more secret books or other items hidden in the apartment.

All she found was a longing to start the next chapter of their life.

Ellice, in her excitement for what was to come, didn't allow herself that moment of grief and dread that always came when she thought of the future. With the book by her side, she vowed to find a way to prove herself wrong.

The three of them settled easily into a routine of work and movie nights. And late nights exploring all the pleasures Jonah's body could bring her.

And the occasional training session when he had to work Saturdays. The computer business really was booming. Every Saturday night when he returned with some exciting new story or discovery, Ellie knew what it meant.

The future Ellice pictured without Cora was hurtling ever toward them.

She could tell Cora felt her sense of urgency about mastering all her Gifts—of which now consisted the Ability to Move Objects, the Talking to Animals (that one had come as quite the surprise when a pigeon squawked at her to get the hell away from its breadcrumbs) and one they simply called Touch. It seemed Ellice's Sight not only worked as a lie detector and future predictor, but if she held an object in her hand, it told of the past. Hence, 'Touch.'

Yes, Cora could tell Ellice was frantically scrambling toward some end goal. She just didn't know what that goal was.

And Ellie vowed to keep it that way.

One day, on the not so rare anymore Saturday when Jonah had to work, Cora was less interested in honing Ellice's Move Objects skill as she was in one of her many occult magazines. She sat there, scratching at her cuticles like she always did when she was worried, reading the same page over and over. When Ellie tried to Move the magazine out of Cora's hand, her death grip nearly ripped the pages in half and Ellie stopped.

"What in the world is so fascinating in that magazine?" Ellie asked in exasperation.

More fascinating than this?

She Moved the salt and pepper shakers from the kitchen and threatened to dump both over Cora's head.

Cora swatted them away and sighed.

"You're not gonna like it."

The shakers fell to the ground.

Ellice moved to the easy chair and chewed on her lip.

What has she found out?

"I've been researching." Cora's most powerful three words.

They usually meant some new wondrous Gift for Ellice to explore. Some unfathomable cosmic power for her to harness.

Or... a creepy old book that did an unspeakable thing to Ellice.

From the look on Cora's face, she knew it was the latter.

"Spill it," she said, taking a sip of her water. Magic made her thirsty as hell.

"You're not gonna like it."

"You said that part already."

Cora closed the magazine and flipped it over to the back page where all the advertisements were. "Yeah, but you're *really* not gonna like this."

She pointed to one particular ad that had been circled in blue ink, then red marker atop that.

Wow, this is serious.

The ad read, 'Strange things happening around you? Not sure how to control them? We have the answers. Call...'

Ellice tossed the magazine back to Cora. "No way."

Cora frowned and her eyes flicked to the clock.

Before Ellice could ask what she was up to, there was a knock on the door.

"WHAT DID YOU DO?" ELLICE didn't move to answer the knock, which sounded again.

Cora got up and crossed the apartment toward the door, careful to stay out of Ellice's reach. "What you're too scared to. You need answers, Ellice, and she has them."

The door swung open.

Ellice wasn't sure if Cora had actually opened it, and by the look on Cora's face, neither was she.

Before them stood a statuesque woman, damn near six feet and dressed in all the gothic finery as one might imagine on a Witch of Olde. Her black-as-their-former-apartment hair coiled around her head, fastened impossibly by one thin sliver of a tree branch. Gold robes draped over her long frame, somehow billowing in the nonbreeze of Jonah's building while never obscuring the woman's ample curves. And they were ample, threatening to spill out over the top of her corset at the slightest movement.

Cora and Ellice stood transfixed. Ellice, who had been seated last she recalled, was now at attention beside Cora.

The woman invited herself in and the door which Cora never opened now closed of its own accord behind her.

She sauntered past Ellice and Cora then turned to face them once more. The girls, having never turned themselves, now faced the woman obediently.

The woman looked them both over then addressed Ellice alone, not bothering to ask which of the two was the one she'd been summoned for.

"I am High Priestess Aldora of the Dawning Light Coven and I have come to aid you in your journey along your Path."

Nothing about her seems very Dawning Light.

Aldora's eyes locked onto Ellice's and without moving her lips Ellice heard, "No, I suppose not."

Ellice felt something tickle in her mind and tried to slam down her Shield.

"We'll work on that," Aldora said and glided through the apartment to the living room. After a quick appraisal of the furniture—and finding it severely lacking—she stood tall in the middle of the room and asked, "Now, what exactly are we working with here?"

A weight that Ellice hadn't noticed before lifted off her chest and she found herself once again able to speak.

Though she didn't wish to.

Cora, on the other hand, had exactly the wrong thing to say. "This is Ellice... Craig... and she's a witch."

Aldora waved a hand to cut her off, and Cora's mouth closed. Ellice could sense the weight back beside her and knew Cora couldn't utter a single word if she tried.

The distance between Ellice and Aldora closed, though Ellice hadn't moved nor perceived any movement from the woman. "So you think you're a witch, do you?"

Ellice shook her head.

Aldora glared at her and Ellice felt compelled to speak.

"She thinks I am," Ellice half lied. Yes, Cora was the one who insisted that Ellice was a witch, but try as she had for the past three months, she could find no other explanation.

The High Priestess and Cora closed in on each other much the same as she'd done with Ellice. Aldora looked Cora over and let her thin lips curl into something resembling a smile. "Smart girl, this one."

With the woman's attention now fixed on Cora, Ellice summoned a courage she couldn't muster for herself. "I'm sorry to have wasted your time Ms....tress Aldora?" Ellice fumbled the last part but kept going. "But I'm not a witch. I'm... nothing. Just a woman whose little sister has a wild imagination."

Ellice inched closer to Cora and took her hand. It was on fire.

High Priestess Aldora didn't buy the act one bit. With a sniff of the air and a quick glance around the apartment—Ellice hadn't been able to stop herself from brightening up the place with more enormously blooming flowers—the woman huffed. Then she moved toward the window and said, "Fine whether we're having today... or *you're* having, rather."

"I don't want any trouble," Ellice blurted out.

Aldora's demeanor changed, only slightly, and she glided back to the girls.

Ellice instinctively shoved Cora behind her.

Aldora's voice dripped with sugar now. "I don't want any trouble either. I only wish to help."

Ellice *wanted* to think that nothing felt further from the truth, but she had wiped her mind clean.

The High Priestess nodded in approval. "There's hope for you yet." She pulled a red pen from her robe's inner pocket and scrawled an address on Ellie's palm. The ink sunk in like a tattoo, then disappeared. "We meet every Sunday. Circle starts at dusk. I expect to see you there."

And with that, she was gone.

Cora wiped and scrubbed at Ellice's hand for the next hour but the ink remained. It was part of her now. She didn't say as much to Cora, but she Saw the Circle. Saw the women—and one man—gathered round it with their arms held to the sky. And she Saw herself there, in the middle of the Circle, crying.

"You can't go," Cora said. Ellice didn't have to peek inside to See that she regretted everything.

But, try as she may to fight the part of her that wanted to obey Cora's plea, she knew this was the answer.

Whatever happened to her was of no consequence as long as the High Priestess helped her save Cora.

"I must."

LATE THAT NIGHT, ELLIE felt a sense of finality that she couldn't shake, even as she lay in bed with Jonah. Both exhausted, they still had yet to go to sleep without first making love. No matter what was on her mind, she wouldn't be the one to break their streak.

Jonah's head was on her chest, his hand venturing down below the waistband of her shorts. She'd been so caught up in her worries, she hadn't noticed.

Now, with the sensation of his warm fingers where they've never been, her attention snapped back to the present. She let out a gasp.

Jonah looked back at her with a wild look in his eyes. "I've been dying to...try something."

Ellie pushed her thoughts to the side and scooted her body higher until Jonah's fingers hovered above her mound. She looked down at him with a grin and licked her lips. "Just remember, what goes around comes around."

She didn't exactly know what she was threatening...or promising by his reaction, but her mind had been wandering a lot lately and coming up with some great ideas. If she didn't have all this magic stuff to worry about, his body would have been the only thing on her mind all day.

"Can't wait."

Jonah pushed himself onto his knees and scooted down until he was positioned between Ellie's legs. Instead of removing her shorts and entering her, he pushed them aside and began rubbing his thumb over her. The sensation instantly woke something inside Ellie, causing a moan to escape her lips.

With this show of approval, Jonah's movements became more confident. One finger slid slowly inside as his thumb kept circling.

Ellie found herself moving with him in ways she hadn't before. Her hips thrust up of their own accord and her back arched, pushing herself closer to him.

When she thought she couldn't take it any longer, she suddenly felt two new sensations. The wet slick of Jonah's mouth on her, and the pressure of a second finger working its way inside her.

Ellie let out a sharp breath followed by a long ragged moan.

Until now, their lovemaking had been wonderful, if still a bit unsure and nervous. But the intensity of what he was doing to her body left no room for modesty. Ellie felt something in her break free with every stroke, every lick.

Ellie had to put the pillow over her face to keep from screaming. When she couldn't take it any longer, she slammed her legs shut, forcing Jonah to stop. He tried to spread her legs again, but she pushed him away.

"I warned you," she said between ragged breaths.

When she'd first said it, she hadn't known what she meant, but now with her insides roiling and begging for relief, she was determined to do the same to him.

Ellie motioned for Jonah to stand up and he obeyed. Her legs were jelly, but she managed to scoot herself to the edge of the bed. She ran her fingers along his waistband the same way he'd done to her. He was already bulging out of the top of his pants. She circled the tip with her thumb.

Slowly she tugged his pants down until it was free and caught it on her tongue. A shock of fear went through her as she realized this was as far as her knowledge would get her. Whatever happened next would be pure instinct. So she cleared her mind and let her body explore his.

She kissed and licked the tip a few times before grabbing him at the base and guiding him into her mouth. She took her time and Jonah moaned deeper with every inch. She had this strong urge to suck, but with his size, she had enough trouble just getting her mouth around him.

When he reached the back of her throat, she gagged and had to pull back, but she tried again...and again until she was able to hold him there. Even with him as far as she could manage, there was still so much of him left.

She squeezed him and moved her hand along with her mouth. She only got in a few strokes like this before he was the one jerking back. At first, Ellie thought she'd done it wrong. Then he growled and picked her up.

Nearly tossing her onto the bed, he was on top of her in an instant, then inside her just as fast. For the first time, he slid right in without the initial pinch of pain. She was ready for him.

After the first couple frantic thrusts, Jonah seemed to regain his control and slowed to a steady pace. But Ellie found she didn't want that. She liked that she could make him lose composure. She had the power.

Ellie wrapped her legs around Jonah's hip and pulled him in hard. He froze for an instant but she pushed her own hips toward him, grinding until there was no mistaking what she demanded.

Jonah leaned down and kissed her sweetly on the lips before pounding fast and hard until his whole body tensed.

Still breathing hard, he scooted back down and began sucking on her again. When his fingers shoved inside her, she didn't last much longer. This time, she didn't try closing her legs or getting away. She rode the wave of pleasure until she had nothing left.

Chapter Seven

The next evening, after making up some excuse about inventory at the video store, Ellice found herself right where she'd Known she would be.

And strangely, she also found that she wasn't as terrified of the place as she'd expected.

Maybe it was the lush garden surrounding the small white cottage. Or the sound of birds chirping overhead. Or the fact that she couldn't Feel the High Priestess anywhere on the grounds that made her wonder what delights awaited her inside.

So, with not much trepidation, she climbed the numerous concrete stairs and knocked on the lovely blue door with the upside down horseshoe nailed above it.

When the door opened Ellice was greeted by a short, plump, and cheery woman in pale gold robes. In her flowing brown hair was a crown made of twigs and tiny red berries. "Oh, you must be the new Seeker, Ellice. Lovely name. Mine's Fawn. Pleasure to meet you. Come, make yourself at home."

The woman took Ellice's arm and ushered her inside. The door closed on its own, but that seemed perfectly natural to Ellice now.

The interior of the home was filled with small wooden statues and stars with circles around them and little metal bowls that looked like... like?

Cauldrons.

Ah, yes. Cauldrons, like in the fairytales about little old ladies with moles on their noses and rotten red apples. And...?

Witches.

Yes, witches.

Perfectly natural, Ellice thought.

The walls were adorned with the most gorgeous paintings of naked women dancing in forests. Babies being dangled over fires by their chubby little feet. Large red beasts with black horns and massive...

Yes, perfectly natural.

Candles of every color, though mostly black sat atop every inch of every surface. They gave the cottage a lovely warm glow about it.

Ellice finally found her manners. "Your home is quite lovely."

And much larger than seemed possible from the looks of the exterior of the cottage. But that, too, seemed perfectly natural.

"Why, thank you," said the pleasantly plump woman. "But it's not my home. Or rather, not only my home. It belongs to the Coven."

"Yes, of course." Ellice followed the woman through the expansive living room with its wall of wands to the dining room with its wall of tiny little daggers. The table was set with a velvety red cloth with pale gold trim. The same gold of Lady Fawn's robe. How Ellice *knew* to think of her as a Lady she didn't know. But it felt perfectly natural so she did it.

In fact, everything about this home... this Coven... felt perfectly natural to Ellice and she allowed herself to relax.

Go with the flow.

Do what came *naturally.*

That's why, when the temperature in the room changed suddenly and the chatter of the women who had gathered at the table with Ellice and Lady Fawn had ceased, nothing felt out of sorts.

As they dined on the finest of fruits and vegetables and the large boar with a shiny red apple in its mouth, Ellice didn't notice how she could never quite see the perimeter of the room. When she excused herself to find the restroom, Lady Fawn followed right behind her, and only the narrow pathway to her destination revealed itself.

Back at the long dining table, if she turned her head to her right—which she found she couldn't but thought nothing of—she was certain she wouldn't see High Priestess Aldora. And she was equally certain she wouldn't see the regal woman whispering to a broad man in a red robe the same color of the wine and the tablecloth and Aldora's. And above all else, she wouldn't Know that the man in question would be none other than High Priest Draigh himself.

No, she wouldn't See any such thing.

PROMPTLY AT DUSK, THE grand clock in the hall chimed a deep somber tone and everyone at the table stood at once, including Ellice.

They all glided out the back door, which opened onto an enchanted forest that stretched farther than her eyes could see. Or See.

In the middle of that forest was a black soil clearing the size of a football field. Yet as Ellice stepped down into it, she felt as if she were snuggled into a warm hug from someone dear. Someone... familiar.

In the center of the cozy field was a large Circle of gray stone, big enough for several—thirteen to be exact—people to stand comfortably around. Ellice somehow Knew the stones were far more ancient than anything known to man, even much older than the *book* that had found her through Cora. The name of which she now Knew was a Grimoire.

And Ellice *knew* she was the thirteenth member this Coven had been waiting for.

High Priestess Aldora and High Priest Draigh stood together at the top of the Circle, where Ellice innately knew was North.

Ellice found herself standing *around* the circle, surrounded by her new Sisters. Not inside it. Not crying as she'd Seen.

And for that, she was grateful.

Aldora raised her arms skyward as Ellice had Seen, but this no longer struck fear in her heart.

"We call to the North, that which breathes Air into our lives and gives us purpose."

As Aldora spoke the words, in a long slow motion Draigh blew a whistling wind into the stone of the North corner.

The air above the Circle chilled and Ellice nestled closer to Lady Fawn.

As if on cue, the entire Coven walked clockwise—deosil—around the Circle. Ellice no longer questioned how she *knew* such things.

When the High Priestess and Priest were positioned over the East corner of the Circle, Aldora's voice rose once more. "We call to the East, that which binds us to the Earth and guides us upon our Path."

Draigh produced a cauldron, slightly larger than the ones Ellice had noticed upon entering the cottage, and placed it atop the prehistoric gray stone of the East corner.

Again the Coven moved with solemn purpose around the Circle until the High Priestess and Priest were standing over the South corner.

"We call to the South, that which burns like Fire within our hearts and makes us Whole once more."

With a flick of his finger, a blue flame burst to light on Draigh's thumb, which he placed upon a white candle on the South stone.

Ellice's own palm itched with the familiar blue lightning but she scraped it away on the side of her jeans. She wished she had a lovely pale golden robe like her Sisters and instantly felt it surround her. She reveled in its warmth.

Yet again, the Coven moved as one around the Circle until the High Priestess and Priest were at the West corner.

"We call to the West, that which quenches our thirst for knowledge and drowns our sorrows with Water from the heavens."

This time, Draigh nodded to the woman at his side, Lady Rain. And as her name aptly predicted, a light shower formed over one stone and one stone only. That of the West corner.

"Now," Aldora nearly sang to her Sisters as she moved to the center of the Circle.

Ellice willed the High Priestess not to call her into the center, and she did not.

"Now, we invite our newest Sister to bless us with her Name."

All eyes were upon Ellice and she feared she had no answer. But as if from the depths of her soul, one came forth.

"Sky."

"Welcome, Lady Sky," came the voice of all her Sisters and one Brother at once.

Chapter Eight

After the ritual, which also included an Anointment of Lady Esme and Handfasting of two other Sisters, the crowd settled and started to disperse.

Ellice didn't feel much like leaving and instead lingered near the dining table. The events of the day had left her famished, and she nibbled on the hind bits of the roasted boar.

Aldora's voice whispered in her ear. "I see you're more amenable to our hospitalities now."

Ellice knew the High Priestess was smiling without having to turn to her side.

"Yes, thank you. It was quite a lovely ceremony." She popped a cherry tomato in her mouth.

Strange. She could have sworn she hated the bitter little things.

"Although," she continued, finding her train of thought once more. "I didn't expect to be so...included on my first visit."

Aldora flicked the thought away. "One normally wouldn't be. However, you will be quite the protégé I suspect. So, why bother with such... formalities?"

And you're much nicer than the first time we met.

Aldora's mood shifted ever so slightly, though the meaning behind it flitted away like a forgotten dream. "One must keep up appearances when out in public, you know."

"Yes," Ellice agreed.

Such a perfectly natural explanation.

THAT EVENING, THE FARTHER Ellice got from the quaint little cottage, the less she remembered about the goings on inside it.

So, when she entered the apartment and Jonah asked how inventory went, she just shrugged and said, "Fine."

And even later, when Jonah was out of earshot and Cora begged for details, Ellice had none to give.

Cora's mood darkened.

Ellice knew her sister thought she was holding out, but truthfully, she had no memory of the afternoon's events. All she was left with was a warm, yet uncomfortable feeling.

And all she could give Cora by way of explanation was, "I think I'm one of them now."

Chapter Nine

And so it went for several months.

Jonah continued to work Saturdays, the 'tech boom' as he called it becoming ever more booming.

Ellice continued to have 'inventory' every Sunday evening, returning home with no clue as to what she'd been doing for the past three to five hours.

Cora continued to grow ever more despondent over the lack of gossip.

And angry. So very angry.

At Ellice.

At the damned woman who pushed her way into their lives and stole her sister.

And at the world for... everything.

The more Ellice pried, the more quiet Cora grew.

Still—and this would be the biggest regret of her life—Ellice didn't try to See what was truly wrong with Cora. She didn't look harder at the increasingly worrisome book collection beside the couch. She didn't notice the dark circles under Cora's eyes until it was too late. She thought she was doing the right thing, letting Cora do her own thing, trusting she would take care of herself.

She was wrong.

Ellice, for her part, tried and mostly succeeded to wall off the section of her mind that worried about the future. About whether Cora would be in it. And about why she didn't remember what she and her other Sisters had been up to.

She knew it was perfectly natural, whatever it was, and she *knew* it was the only way to secure the future she wanted. The one with Jonah *and* Cora.

She still made time to practice her Skills with Cora every Saturday, which always eased the tension between them enough to get them through Sunday.

"Try to reach the lamppost over there," Cora said on one such Saturday, pointing to the one all the way across the *other* street.

"You've got to be kidding."

"Come on. The last one could've easily hit it." Cora squeezed Ellice's arm but quickly released it. They'd found out the hard way what happened if anyone was touching Ellice when she used certain Gifts.

With a sigh, Ellice pushed up her sleeves. They held no bearing on her power, but Cora was a sucker for theatrics.

She stared at her hands, willing the blue lightning to the surface. It flowed with ease now and in a breath of a second, Ellice flung it out through the gray sky. It hit the target dead on and they were rewarded with a loud bang before the street plunged into darkness.

If Ellice had been paying attention, she would have noticed that this darkness had the same intensity as the one in her old apartment. But she'd long since forgotten all about that fateful evening.

Besides, it had brought her closer to Jonah and there couldn't be anything wrong with that.

ELLIE'S NEW ROSY OUTLOOK on life also had much to do with the progression of her relationship with Jonah.

One Friday night in particular, he had insisted that they dress up and go out to this fancy restaurant one of the guys at the office had suggested.

Ellie knew what was coming, had dreamt about this night for months. Though her Sight had failed her where her own future was concerned, the writing was on the wall.

They rarely left each other's side these days, aside from the call of his beloved tech boom and her duties as the new manager of the video rental store.

And of course her Sunday inventory, an alibi that now made more sense given her greater responsibilities.

Something nagged at Ellie at the thought of that word.

Responsibilities.

She'd done everything possible to ensure her future with Jonah and Cora would be happy and *long*.

Hadn't she?

Her mind was always a blank slate after her Sunday Circles, but deep down Ellie could feel things shifting. She was growing stronger. She had more control over her Gifts now.

Surely if something bad were coming, she would *know* it.

She looked to Jonah as they entered the restaurant and the room grew dim. But she could still see him. Always. No matter what, he would be there for her. With her.

And nothing would tear them apart.

Certainly not tonight.

Chapter Ten

Jonah had fumbled his way through dinner, barely touching his rare steak and red potatoes. His favorite.

What he did touch, however, was three glasses of wine.

And his side pocket more than several times as if making sure something—*it*—was still there.

Not much for drinking normally, his cheeks had flushed along with most of his face, and Ellie could no longer see the cute little freckles she loved so dearly.

But she could see the frantic energy in his eyes, and she loved that more. She loved *him* more than anything.

"I... uh... you know I..." he sputtered. Then he closed his eyes and forced himself to breathe.

"I love you, too." She reached across the table and touched his burning cheek.

His eyes opened, and the breath heaved out of him. "I love you so much Ellie Bellie. This past year has been the best time of my whole life."

A year already?

"... never thought I'd find a girl... woman... as perfect as you. Or that you'd ever be with the likes of me."

"Shh, don't talk like that." Ellie hated when Jonah talked down about himself. To her, *he* was the perfect one. Her knight in shining armor if she believed in such things.

Jonah reached into his coat pocket and pulled out a red velvet box. He creaked it open, exposing a tiny but perfect engagement ring.

"It's beautiful," Ellie whispered.

Tears that had been waiting for him to finally say those four words could wait no longer. They fell freely as he pulled the ring out of its box and held it up to her.

"Ellie Bellie, will you marry me?"

OK, six words.

But Ellie didn't care. "Yes! Yes, of course I will. Oh, I was wondering what was taking you so long!"

She let him slip the ring on her finger before jumping up and kissing him with a rekindled passion that burned bright in her core.

They made fevered love that night.

And every night after, for the month it took to make arrangements.

Jonah didn't know all the sordid details of her past, but he knew enough to not ask for a big ceremony. They discretely married at the courthouse with Cora as their witness.

And that night, when they made slow love like their first time, Ellie felt like she'd come home.

As he moved inside her, she dug her nails into his back.

When her soft moans filled the air, he plunged deeper, losing himself within her.

When she felt his release, and her clutching explosion soon after, she thought of how she wanted—needed for every night of the rest of her life to be just like this one.

Later, as he softly snored beside her, Ellie felt something else the core of her being.

Something new, yet utterly familiar.

Something she already loved more than even her Jonah.

Much later, Ellie would tell her daughter—for she *knew* it was a girl—of the night she was conceived.

Of course, she'd leave out most of the story, only filling her daughter's heart with the love of the father she would never know.

Chapter Eleven

Things changed quickly and drastically after that next Sunday.

As soon as she entered the small cottage that always became much more on the inside, Ellice felt every eye upon her.

Lady Fawn, now less of a shadow and more the Sister she was meant to be, rushed to Ellie's side and laid a plump little hand upon her belly.

Ellie's cheeks burned.

So much for keeping this to myself.

The Sisters gathered around her, no need for words. They all Knew.

High Priestess Aldora glided into the room as she was known to do and placed her long slender hand where Lady Fawns had suddenly ceased to be.

Ellie felt a quiver of movement.

No. That can't be.

But the High Priestess felt it too. She jerked her hand back in a swift motion and ordered everyone to the Circle.

They hurried to their places and Aldora didn't waste time calling the corners.

They didn't even wait for High Priest Draigh who was nowhere to be found.

"Sisters, we are gathered here today to bear witness to the Blessed Gift bestowed upon one of our very own by the Goddess Herself. This child shall be our Future, our Destiny, our way Onward into the Light."

"THAT WAS WEIRD," ELLIE had said on her way home that night. Though just *what* was weird, she couldn't recall.

"Darling!" Jonah called the moment she opened the door. He'd taken to calling her that sometimes since their wedding night and she found she didn't hate it. It was better than Ellie Bellie, though sometimes she found herself missing the pet name.

Ellie met him in the middle of the apartment where he'd nearly run to meet her.

"I've got fabulous news!" He could barely contain himself as he ushered her to the couch and made her sit.

Ellie couldn't help but think of the news she, too, had for him. Fabulous as it also was, five days was way too soon to spring it on him. How would she ever explain *knowing* that?

Ellice looked to Cora for some insight, but Cora—who she did tell right away and who had reacted in the exact opposite way as Ellice had expected—gave no hint as to what was coming. She barely lifted her eyes from yet another black and ominous looking book she'd taken to reading all day every day.

Her sister's eyes had become more sunken and dark circled with each passing month. Her skin had shriveled, or more like her entire body had shriveled beneath her skin. Already thin to begin with, Ellice couldn't help but liken her to a skeleton.

Jonah's excited words broke into her thoughts. "Isn't that great?"

Ellie blinked, trying to force some recess of her mind—and her Mind—to recall what he'd been saying.

"It means way more money for us. We can get out of this tiny apartment and buy our own big house. Get Cora her own room. You'd like that wouldn't you, Cora?" he asked brightly toward the corner of the apartment. If he'd also noticed Cora wasting away to nothing, he'd never once said.

A muffled, "Mmhmm," was all that came from the sullen corner.

"Well, I'm excited," Jonah continued without missing a beat. "Aren't you excited?"

"So excited," Ellie answered, willing as much enthusiasm as she could into her voice.

She didn't tell him—couldn't tell him—what was really on her mind that night.

He would never make it long enough to know what it was like to live in a nice house with new furniture.

Or watch his daughter grow up in that house.

Chapter Twelve

When the baby came, Ellice was on her knees in the middle of the Circle. It had only been seven months. It was too soon.

Way too soon.

But there was no time.

In the midst of all the pain and fear, Ellice remembered the vision she'd had long ago.

Her in the middle of the Circle, crying.

She had been standing in the vision, but she *knew* this was the moment. It had all come together.

But why hadn't she seen the swollen belly?

"It's too soon," she moaned, clutching the bottom of her stomach, begging the child inside to stay.

Just a little while longer.

She wouldn't make it another two months, but she could at least make it to a hospital. She reached for the High Priestess or Lady Fawn, or someone *anyone* to help her.

But they all stood back, waiting and watching.

Only High Priest Draigh came to her.

His wine red robe was tied behind him, looking more like a cape, but he didn't feel like any hero to Ellice.

His green eyes shone bright with a fire Ellice had never seen in him before. He'd always seemed so kind and helpful, even *meek* at times despite his size, deferring to Aldora at every turn.

But now, he was in charge and Ellice would only be leaving this Circle with a baby in her arms.

Her mind ached with the flash of a different Circle. The only other time High Priest Draigh had been in command. But the thought flitted away like a cool breeze as her stomach clamped down on the baby.

She was coming soon. Ellice's body knew what to do, and did so even against Ellice's will.

"It's time," said Draigh.

"No," begged Ellice.

Now, Aldora and the women who didn't feel like Sisters any longer closed ranks around her.

The moment they all stepped within the bounds of the Circle, the last thread of Ellice's womb tore itself loose.

She screamed in agony as a wave of contractions crashed through her.

Lady Moon was the only one kind enough, or brave enough, to approach her. She lifted Ellice's skirts, though Ellice tried to stop her, and rubbed a foul smelling salve on the swollen parts of her.

Blissfully, the ripping sensation eased a bit, though the salve had done nothing for the tight clawing force within her. Ellice's body was determined to expel this baby.

And the child, Ellice *knew* was eager to emerge.

So she let go.

Draigh moved between her legs and flung Ellice's robe aside. For now, without knowing how, Ellice was clad in a white robe and nothing more.

She had the absurd thought of getting it filthy from the ground she lay upon as the world around her dimmed.

At the crest of the next contraction, she drifted into a warm dark nothing.

The peace only lasted a second before Ellice snapped to.

Draigh's hands were plunged deep within the place they didn't belong.

But she no longer cared.

Of course it was perfectly natural for him to be here with her. With them.

Perfectly natural.

"Bring me a towel," Draigh ordered and this time it was High Priestess Aldora who followed orders. She sprang into action, disappearing and reappearing in an instant with a pure white cotton baby blanket.

Draigh took it from her and Ellice saw blood, her blood, oozing between his fingers.

So much blood.

But that was perfectly natural, wasn't it?

One can't deliver the Light without getting a little bloody, can they?

The Light.

Something about those words felt wrong.

Dangerous.

Ellice forced herself to rouse, to see—and See—what was happening to her. To her baby.

Through the haze, Draigh's large brooding figure leaned over her. He was doing something… something painful and *wrong*.

Then, with one final contraction and a heavy tug from Draigh, there came a release. And relief.

Everyone moved inward at once, crowding around the baby.

For a moment, everyone held their breath.

When the tiny cry finally rang out into the night, it was followed by the exhales of the entire Coven.

High Priest Draigh cleaned the baby with the corner of the white blanket and held her up for all to see.

All but Ellice, who had been forgotten.

She lay in the middle of the Circle bleeding and still writhing in pain. One more brutal contraction pushed itself down on her and she felt something slick and hot between her legs.

In the recesses of her mind, she realized this was the placenta, but she didn't care.

All she cared about was her baby. And that port-wine stain birthmark on her inner left thigh. She was not one for superstition, but she knew all too well what those meant. Her precious baby had been a fierce warrior in a past life and she'll not escape that fate in this one.

Ellice tried to stand but fell back, hitting her head on the hard ground.

Nobody paid her any mind, except for Lady Fawn. She broke away from the crowd and came toward Ellice.

Thinking her Sister was coming to offer comfort, Ellice reached out her arms.

But Lady Fawn only produced a pair of scissors from her robe and cut the umbilical cord, severing Ellice's link with her daughter.

The next few moments passed in a blur. Ellice could have sworn there was dancing and chanting all around her, though she could barely stay conscious to hear *what* her Coven was saying to her daughter.

Before giving in to the twilight of sleep, Ellice thought she heard High Priestess Aldora say, "We will call her Freyja."

But that wasn't the name she and Jonah had picked for their daughter.

With her final clear thought, she knew what had felt so wrong since the day she stepped foot in the cottage.

Freyja was the one they had been waiting for, not Ellice.

Chapter Thirteen

Ellie awoke in a hospital bed, frantically searching the covers for her baby.

She dimly remembered hushed voices that grew louder and more urgent. Something about blood loss and the sound of sirens.

Where is she?

"Where's my baby?" Ellie screamed.

"Here! Here..." Jonah's soothing voice pulled her from her nightmare, for she was sure that's all it was.

Perfectly natural for a new mother to have nightmares about losing her baby.

Right?

Jonah placed the warm bundle of blankets in Ellie's arms and bright green eyes stared wide back at her.

"Gave us quite a scare, darling." Jonah sat in the plastic chair beside her hospital bed. "We're sure lucky those nice women were coming back from church and found you. Who knows what would've happened if you and Sarah had been out there much longer."

Sarah.

Yes, that's the name we picked for our daughter.

Ellie looked around the room to find the rest of it empty. "Where's Cora?"

"Hmm." Jonah scanned the room as well. "After the doctors said everything was alright with you and the baby, she said she had something to take care of." He shrugged and smiled at her. "Probably went down to the gift shop to clean them out of every pink thing they have."

"Yes, you're probably right," Ellie replied, though she didn't believe it.

Cora was in danger. Her bones ached with the *knowing* of it.

AGAINST DOCTOR'S ORDERS, and Jonah's begging, Ellie signed herself out of the hospital that night.

She took Sarah home, fed her and rocked her, and cried as the baby slept in her arms.

Then she cried over Jonah's sleeping form as she kissed him on the forehead and said her goodbyes.

Maybe the reason she never saw their future wasn't because he and Cora were gone, but because *she* was gone.

Ellie couldn't bear the thought of her sweet baby girl growing up without a mother and she'd do everything in her Powers to keep that from happening.

But Cora was her sister and she had to save her.

It wasn't easy walking all the way to the cottage, especially not in her condition. But as dawn approached, Ellie knocked hard on the drab blue door.

It swung open.

Ellice had tried the whole way here to *feel* Cora and never could.

Now, as her eyes adjusted to the darkness inside the cottage, she knew why.

Cora was on the floor. Blood pooled beneath her and there was a strong odor of burnt flesh assaulting Ellie's senses.

She rushed to her sister and clamped her hands down hard on the girl's side. She'd never tried to use her healing on anything more than plants and a big toe, but it was all she could think to do.

The blue light sputtered to her palms and soaked into the hole in Cora's abdomen.

"Stop that this instant!" Aldora's voice cut through Ellice's concentration like a knife.

The woman stood far across the room, yet her words felt like they came from inside Ellice's head.

She shook them loose and continued pushing her Power into Cora, begging it to hurry up!

Aldora didn't waste more time with words.

Ellice flew through the air and slammed with a deafening thud against the wall of wands.

Several fell around her and she picked one up, pointing it at Aldora's chest.

But nothing happened. They were just for show.

"Where is she?" This time it was Draigh whose voice penetrated her mind.

"You'll never see her again!" Ellice flung the useless wand and held out her hands toward Draigh. The blue light flickered and extinguished, spent from trying to save Cora.

Trying.

It wasn't enough. She hadn't been strong enough.

"No," Aldora agreed, this time speaking normally. "But it's of no consequence. *She's* of no consequence. What is one girl in the grand scheme of things?"

"My sister!" Ellice roared and a dagger from the dining room wall soared through the air.

It narrowly missed Aldora's head as the High Priestess moved ever so slightly to the side and waved her hand.

A red-hot ball of fire hurled toward Ellice.

She rolled out of the way, positioning herself between Cora and the onslaught of fire and gusting wind that had begun to swirl inside the cottage.

If there was even the slightest chance, she had to try.

Draigh lunged for her, covering the expanse of the cottage in no time. "Bring her to us! She is ours!"

"Never!"

Draigh grabbed Ellice by the throat and picked her up high into the air. Her hair brushed the ceiling and her feet flailed beneath her, searching for something to cling to. What they found instead, was Draigh's crotch, which served just as well.

He dropped her and she tumbled back to the floor, landing beside Cora and instinctively covering her sister with her own body.

"Enough of this nonsense!" Aldora came forward.

In the split second before the High Priestess was upon her, Ellice heard the softest whisper.

Should have killed her when I had the chance.

Ellice's head snapped back.

Aldora froze. It was only a moment, the shock of dropping her Shield causing her to falter.

It was all Ellice needed.

Still shielding Cora with her body, she willed one of the wands to rise from the floor and fling itself directly into Aldora's left eye.

The High Priestess crumbled, screaming in an agony that reminded Ellice of the pain she'd been in mere hours before. Right there in the back yard where none of her Sisters had lifted a finger to help her.

With a huff of anger and a twitch of her head, the wand twisted itself deeper into Aldora's eye socket.

The High Priestess went limp.

Ellice rubbed her hands together and placed them back on Cora's side.

"Come on, work damn you!"

Then suddenly she thought she felt something. A stirring perhaps? Or a flinch of pain?

But Cora didn't stir.

No!

A massive hand grabbed Ellice's hair and yanked her up, back into the air. But this time, she was only high enough to be face to face with

Draigh, who seemed to be no longer affected by the blow to his manhood.

"Give me what is mine and I will bring your friend back."

He was lying. He'd never once shown any abilities in Life magic.

Still, if there was even a chance.

"Her first," Ellice demanded.

With a vicious howl that emanated from somewhere outside his body, Draigh sucked in a long breath.

It took only a second for Ellice to realize that the air filling his lungs was coming from hers. She gasped and clawed at his hands.

She couldn't die, not like this. Not with her dear Jonah and Sarah at home waiting for her.

Not with Cora's body covered in blood with nobody left to mourn her after I'm gone.

Draigh stopped draining the life from Ellice long enough to say, "This is your last warning."

He immediately returned to pulling the breath from her, which didn't feel like much of a warning.

Ellice scrambled for what to do next. Her eyes darted around the room, begging for something sharp or heavy to hurl at Draigh's head. But all she saw were stars.

Just as the last star began to fade, Ellice heard a loud crash and Draigh's grip on her hair loosened. The air being sucked out of her returned at once and she gasped as she fell again to the floor beside Cora.

Only this time, Cora was not laying dead in her own blood. She was propped against an end table, reaching for something above her head.

Ellice saw that it was one of the many candles in the cottage about the same time as she smelled the smoke. Beneath it was the fresh stench of newly burned flesh.

She risked a fleeting glance back at Draigh. His clothes were covered in flames. The oxygen he'd been stealing from her had turned him into a powder keg.

Cora threw another candle in his direction and it collided with the growing wall of fire surrounding him.

For as long as she lived, Ellice would never forget that whooshing sound.

The fire engulfing Draigh danced over him, leaping from one side of the room to the next, then to the ceiling.

"Come on, we have to get out of here. Now!" Ellice took Cora's arm and pulled with all she had left, but her sister slumped back against the table.

"I can't. Go. You go." Cora's voice was nothing more than a breath.

"No, I won't. I can't leave you!"

"You have to. You have a daughter now. A family." Cora's head rolled to the side.

"No!" Ellice tried to lift Cora again but couldn't. "You're my family," she pleaded. "You're my family."

Cora didn't answer. Ellice could see her chest still rising, faintly.

"Why aren't you helping me?" Ellice wanted to grab Cora by the shoulders and shake her. Grind her hands into the hole on her side. Anything to force the fight back into her.

The smoke that had once been high above them was now thick and low, coating Ellice's throat and lungs.

When Cora didn't respond even to the hot air that should have choked her, Ellice knew she was letting go.

Cora was giving up.

Ellice covered her mouth and nose with her shirt, then did the same for Cora.

Then, she did the one thing she'd sworn never to do.

She read her sister's mind.

Chapter Fourteen

Cora's mind, which had once been full of fairytales and wonder, was now an empty void. Nothing was left but one dim light in the center, quickly being devoured by the darkness.

But beneath the vast quiet, was a whisper of jumbled thoughts.

All my fault. My fault.

Should have tried harder.

Couldn't save you.

"No!" Ellie screamed into the void. "It's not your fault. You didn't know."

Wasn't strong enough.

Should have left me on the Row.

Would've been safer.

"No, Cora. Come on. Come back to me! I need you!"

Deserve this...

Too late. I was too late.

The book...

The light flickered out.

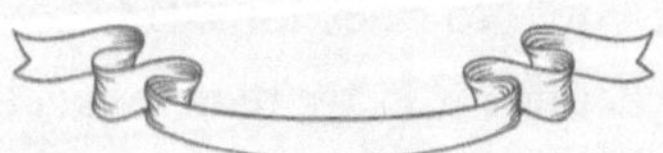

ELLICE HAD STAYED WITH Cora, even as the cottage burned around them.

Only when she saw Aldora's lifeless body begin to rise, did she pull herself up and let go of her sister's hand.

The sun had moved across the sky and now hung bright and taunting high above her as Ellie made her way back to the apartment.

Jonah, who had been looking through the peephole as usual, flung the door open and rushed to her.

"Where have you been? What... what's wrong? Are you hurt?" A flurry of questions followed her as she took the baby from his arms and wrapped her in a bedsheet and tied it over her shoulder.

"Why do you smell like smoke? Whose blood is that?"

"Cora's." It was the only question she deemed worth a response.

"What? Ellie, darling, what's going on? Please talk to me." Jonah tried to stop her from pulling steak knives from the kitchen drawer but she jerked away. "Come on, Ellie Bellie, you're scaring me."

Sarah squirmed in the bundle of sheets, sensing the fear and tension clouding the room.

Ellie patted her bottom and she quieted. When the pain of that motion caused Ellie's hands to curl into fists, she took precious seconds they didn't have to wrap them.

She'd pushed herself too far, and for what?

"There's no time to explain everything. I need you to trust me. Do as I say and don't question any of it." Ellie couldn't believe she was about to say this next part but she had to give him the option. "Or stay and let me take her to safety."

"Safety? What the... Ellie what have you gotten yourself into?"

Ellie moved past him and headed for the door. "No questions."

"OK, okay, I trust you. No questions." He took her in his arms and pulled her to him. "Whatever it is, we're in it together."

Ellie allowed herself five seconds to feel the comfort he was trying to give her. Then she stepped back toward the door. "We need a place to hide."

Chapter Fifteen

The only place either of them could come up with was his office.

It was downtown, in the middle of all the hustle and bustle of city life that had once brought her so much joy. Now, it was nothing more than an escape plan.

Hide in plain sight.

With all the people hurrying about, Aldora would never be able to pick up her trail.

As they rushed off the train and up the subway stairs, Jonah said, "And we have guards!"

She'd told him the necessary bits on the train. About her Gifts—though they didn't seem like gifts now. About the Coven and the fire.

And Cora.

But mostly she'd been silent. Planning their next move. And Jonah had let her be.

Clearly he was in shock and Ellie expected that once it wore off, he'd have plenty more questions.

She only hoped they both lived long enough for that conversation.

In the end, they both still agreed that his office building would be the safest place.

And they almost made it, too.

"DON'T TAKE ANOTHER step."

Aldora appeared from around the corner, a crude bandage wrapped around her eye and charred flesh on both her hands.

Ellie put a hand instinctively over the bundle wrapped around her chest.

Jonah, also on instinct, put himself between his family and the woman.

No.

Ellie wanted to move, to warn him, or get in front of him. But she could only stand there and hold the bundle tighter as a ball of fire caught Jonah in the arm.

He stumbled backward into her, but stayed upright. "Leave my family alone!"

"You can keep her," Aldora said, gesturing toward Ellie. "All I want is Freyja."

Ellice hadn't had time or the wherewithal to mention that part and Jonah's head snapped back in confusion.

When the bundle squirmed at the name she clearly recognized, Ellie knew Jonah had figured it out as well.

"Not a chance," he yelled back at her.

All the while, they'd been inching their way toward his building. Only two doors stood between them and possible sanctuary.

But Aldora was having none of it.

She moved closer, eyes locked onto the bundle around Ellie's chest. "Give it to me and you live."

Ellie took a large step backward, pulling Jonah with her. "Never!"

One of the knives in her pocket loosed itself and tumbled through the air, taking aim at Aldora's good eye.

Ellie and Jonah took the chance and ran toward the building.

They were so close.

Aldora swiftly avoided the knife and charged for Ellie. Her long fingers clawed at the knot holding Sarah's bundle together.

Rage boiled up inside Ellie. Rage for her daughter, for Cora, for every person this vile woman had ever hurt.

A car lifted off the road and flew at Aldora, knocking her off balance long enough for them to reach the glass doors of Jonah's building.

We made it!

A flash of white slammed into Jonah's back and Ellie heard the breath leaking out of him.

She shoved him inside and as she was scrambling in behind him, something yanked her back.

A strong wind sucked her away from the door, away from Jonah and safety.

Jonah reached for her as she slid back, heels digging into the marble walkway. She watched him stumble to the ground, clutching the bundle that held her sweet Sarah.

Is that blood?

"When will you ever learn?" Draigh called over the howling wind.

A blast of heat struck her shoulder and knocked her loose from Draigh's hold.

As another ball of fire whirled past her head, Ellie's eyes filled with tears and she did the only thing she could think of.

"What's wrong with your aim? Having a little trouble?" She taunted Aldora as she ran in the opposite direction.

A wicked laugh rose up from somewhere inside her and she let another escape, despite the fury it would bring down upon her.

Chapter Sixteen

White light crashes overhead as Ellice ducks behind the nearest car. The world dulls in its wake. Sound and sensation both fray, leaving her exposed.

No no no no no.

Aldora's voice booms from everywhere at once. "The Goddess has spoken. Return what is ours and you shall live."

Another bright light explodes, nearer this time. Ellice uses the illumination to search for cover up ahead. Overturned cars burn around her. Everything is closing in.

In the distance, she sees a small building that looks like an electrical shed. Probably the worst place to hide, aside from this flimsy Prius that could fly away at any moment.

"Come out before this entire city burns!" This time it's Draigh's deafening howl that cuts through the night.

The whole world will burn before I let you win.

Ellice looks at her bandaged hands, willing them to work one last time. She stretches her aching fingers but nothing happens.

Absently, Ellie feels for the bundle she'd had strapped to her chest. But it's gone. She *knew* it would be, but still she can't stop herself from checking.

No, the bundle is gone now, along with everything else she once held dear.

The next flash of light is tinged with red as it nearly finds its mark. Ellie knows she must run for the building now. But she's frozen.

Jonah!

All she sees is smoke and fire. The building where she left them has disappeared.

Please...

Ellice doesn't know if she's begging Jonah, or the Goddess, or her hands. But these damn hands are the only thing she currently has some control over.

She pushes her back against the car, desperately molding her body to its form.

Blood thrums in her head as she forces a calming breath, then another. On the third, she unwraps the scrap of Jonah's bloody t-shirt from her hands. The pain explodes as burnt flesh tears away with it.

Biting her lip to keep from screaming, she kisses the shirt before letting it drop to the road. It may be the last thing of his she'll ever touch.

Aldora's voice reverberates in Ellice's chest. "I shall not ask again!" She's getting closer. Another blinding flash of white illuminates the sky.

Ellice takes the opportunity to search for Jonah, but to no avail.

I've lost everything. But they won't take me alive.

She returns to her breathing, starting over with one, two, three. She must make it to five. On the fourth, the familiar warm blue glow begins to creep down her forearm.

As smoke fills her lungs on the fifth breath, Ellice rises to her feet and calls out to the darkness. "Your reign is over! There is nothing left for any of us. I'll see you in Hell!"

Ellice's palms burn as blue lightning crackles within them.

I'm sorry I failed you.

Ellice clasps both hands over her heart.

And as the pulse of electricity begins to charge, a large hand clamps down on her shoulder.

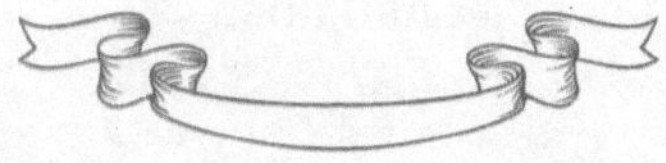

SHE WHIRLS AROUND HOPING her hands are ready to blast her attacker.

"Ellie!"

"Jonah?"

He crouches down beside her, staring at her glowing hands.

It's one thing to hear about magic, and another to see it flying over your head from two crazy assholes. But another still to see it burning under the skin of the woman you love.

"Does it hurt?" he asks, taking her hands in his.

"Where's Sarah? Is she..."

Ellie can't bring herself to ask.

"With the guards," Jonah assured her.

Another flash of white falls even closer to them.

"What can I do?" Jonah asks? "How can I help?"

Ellie stares at him. What *can* he do?

She rips the bottom of her shirt, wads it into a ball, and lights it with her palm.

Jonah takes it from her and tosses it over the car. He rips his shirt and shoves it in her direction.

Ellie crawls around the side of the car and shoots a lightning bolt at Draigh. It catches him on the side of his already charred flesh. Direct hit, but now he knows where they are.

"I'm gonna make a run for that building. You hold them off as long as possible." Ellie lights Jonah's shirt and kisses him hard.

Just in case, she lies to herself.

With the loss of Cora, Ellie is now certain that her inability to see a future with either of them was because they both die, here and now.

She knows without having to See that in Jonah's eyes is the determination of a loving husband and father. He will give his life to protect theirs and she has to let him do it.

For Sarah's sake.

A MOMENT LATER, CROUCHING behind the small electrical station, Ellie watches it all.

The afternoon sky which had somehow gone dark, lights up with one final crash of orange and red.

The wind whips cars and trees and everything not bolted down into the sky.

Including her Jonah.

She doesn't let herself close her eyes as he slams into the front of his office building, shattering the glass and falling limply to the marble walkway. The shards rain down on his unmoving form.

Aldora and Draigh both turn their attention back to Ellie before Jonah heaves out his final breath.

Ellie's gaze is ripped from Jonah's unmoving chest as the two figures barrel toward her. Aldora's arms are outstretched and ready to deal their next fatal blow. Draigh's mouth is open, a black void pulling her to him.

Ellice does not struggle. Does not run.

Red hot rage crowds her field of vision as she charges at both of them.

The next several seconds or minutes fly past in a whir of guttural screams, body parts, and burnt flesh. Her hands around Draigh's neck, blue electricity crawling up his veins. Aldora with a burning hole in her gut, falling hard onto the street below.

When they're no longer a threat, Ellice turns her fury on everything around her. Cars fly through the air and burst into flames high overhead. The small outbuilding she'd tried to seek solace behind explodes. The ground quakes but her feet don't notice. She is no longer tethered to the world.

Ellice shoots to the sky, straight up then straight down, gaining speed. She pushes herself harder, determined to be with her Jonah. A second before she hits, her daughter's innocent face flashes before her eyes.

Her feet skid against nothing and she braces for impact, silently apologizing to her sweet Sarah for her weakness.

Ellice comes to in the lobby of Jonah's old office building with Sarah in her arms.

The guards all give them space as paramedics try to bring Jonah back.

When the long steady beep of their machine doesn't stop ringing in her ears, Ellice looks down into her daughter's green eyes.

And vows to shield her from this cruel world for as long as she has breath left in her body.

To Be Continued...

Awaken; Book One of Shadow Borne

S he is mine.
     I shall have her.
Possess her.

Feel the fire that burns deep within her soul.

It is mine for the taking; yet with that taking comes the relinquishing of my own power. For it is hers to do with as she wills.

And she will do such great things with it. Of that I am sure.

Much time I have wasted, waiting for the perfect moment to strike. A moment I fear may not come in this lifetime if left for the gods to decide.

Too long I've been forced to sit idly by, watching from afar as she gives herself to those who are not worthy. They ken not what gift they hold in their hands. Who they toss aside once their hunger is sated.

Sometimes it is she who casts them out quickly and I wonder, nae pray that it is in those moments she realizes what more she deserves.

What she is capable of achieving, of harnessing!

My own soul, which I shall gladly offer.

Only I can give her what she needs, what she truly desires.

Alas, what I desire.

Yet I have forced myself not to act upon my own base needs until the time comes for us to be together. I feel it is too soon. She may not be ready.

I must wait and watch.

For now.

About Author

Asta Horne is an author and reader of Paranormal Romance. The darker the better! After spending twenty years as a ghostwriter, she decided it was her turn. Now Shadow Borne can finally come out to play. Book One of the series, Awaken[1], is now on pre-order (or live if you're reading this after June 2023).

To keep up with Shadow Borne and upcoming series, please follow Asta on:

Instagram
TikTok
Facebook

---

1. https://www.amazon.com/Awaken-Shadow-Borne-Book-1-ebook/dp/B0C1L21J8S

Don't miss out!

Visit the website below and you can sign up to receive emails whenever Asta Horne publishes a new book. There's no charge and no obligation.

https://books2read.com/r/B-A-UEXY-RSGKC

BOOKS 2 READ

Connecting independent readers to independent writers.